D1649365

Since the Noon Mail Stopped

Johns Hopkins: Poetry and Fiction

John T. Irwin, General Editor

Since the Noon Mail Stopped

Wyatt Prunty

The Johns Hopkins University Press   *Baltimore and London*

HOUSTON PUBLIC LIBRARY

R01056 50465

HUMCA

This book has been brought to publication with the generous assistance of the Albert Dowling Trust and the G. Harry Pouder Fund.

© 1997 The Johns Hopkins University Press
All rights reserved. Published 1997
Printed in the United States of America on acid-free paper

06   05   04   03   02   01   00   99   98   97   5   4   3   2   1

The Johns Hopkins University Press
2715 North Charles Street
Baltimore, Maryland 21218-4319
The Johns Hopkins Press Ltd., London

Some of the poems in this volume were previously published, some in slightly different form, in the following periodicals, to whose editors grateful acknowledgment is made: "Late Fall, Late Light," published as "Fall" in *Boulevard*; "Four Winter Flies," *Formalist*; "Dantini," *Georgia Review*; "Driving the Christmas Lights," *Image*; "The Pyromaniac," *Kenyon Review*; "Etude on a Music Stand" and "Reading before We Read," *New Criterion*; "Grown Men at Touch," *New England Review*; "A Baseball Team of Unknown Navy Pilots, Pacific Theater, 1944" and "Thaumatrope," *New Republic*; "Eyeing the World" and "The Window Washer," *Sewanee Review*; "Golden," *Shenandoah*; "This," "Dog, Dog, Object, Object," "Band Day," and "The God Doll," *Southern Review*; and "Seasons," *Yale Review*. "Coach" appeared in an anthology, *Unleashed* (Crown, 1995).

ISBN 0-8018-5646-9

Library of Congress Cataloging-in-Publication Data will be found at the end of this book.

A catalog record for this book is available from the British Library.

For Peter, Stanley, and Ted

Contents

I

The Sneeze

The first day sleet, the second ice,
And nothing moved, till going for the mail
I stepped, slipped, sailed, heels high, higher,
So blue sky over toes, wide spastic arms,
And shoulder blades blunt anviling the ice—

Where when I hit the spine-long back of me
Some tearing cloth gave out along its seam
As though a child's hand crushed dry cereal.
And then the building cold beneath. Then nothing.

Next I was back and rolling to my side
So right arm down and legs balled tight
I elbowed up. Then wrist-to-hand, tucked feet,
Half stood, balanced, looked around, teetered, slipped;
And it was loose-hinged limp and rubber down.
Lay curled again. Till, knees-to-belly rising,
Feet beneath, I angled up, legs half bent,
Straightened, compassed one way, leaned the other,
Then shuffle-side-stepped, see-saw-armed-it home.

And now for three taut weeks there's been this change:
First eyes tight-sponged and lungs ballooning up

The room inflates, then I am round-eyed huge
As everything I see. And then the sneeze.
And the fine tight grinding mesh goes off again.
Somewhere a small foot scuffs leaves. Goes on.

Seasons

At tennis, a missed shot meant he had MS.
Later, over drinks it was the Big Bands,
Night trains, DC 3's, Packards—an express
Of images held headlong out of hand
In what he called his photogenic memory.
No one corrected. Dinner went well.
But seeing him to his car, he turned to me,
Arms shrugging outward, "What the hell,
Someone stole the Packard. Go call the cops."
Settled in his Buick, window powered down,
He leaned out confidentially, "Dumb slobs,
Putting all this plastic in a Packard."

                          Then he was gone,
And I stood waving, after what? Self-referee
Of a widower and skeptic who when asked
Said, "You believe in clear because it's cloudy."
Ten years alone and nothing of hers packed.
"All charities are scams," he said. "Clear
Us both out all at once. We go together—"
As the Packard or Buick steered a few more years,
Gathering dents inexplicable as weather
And he renamed his tennis, "Rigorous Mortis."

A few late trips; mostly cruises.
But once, a full-blown bash with all the downstairs
Opened wide, bars on porches, in the yard,
And the Big Bands going long past goodnights
And the last few cars turning hard
To clear the drive and accelerate from sight.

House empty, cigar stoked, he went about
Puffing, fly down, shirttail out, blowing smoke
At windowpanes, watching the cloudbanks go,
Each fanning past its glass. Until the last,
In which the smoke resolved him mirrored in
The single pane that told the backward joke
Which, nothing like its small spent storm of dark,
Cleared after him the hall and only stairs
Climbing the whole house rigidly from sight.

The Window Washer

The daily way for looking is inside.
But once a woman glared at him, stripped herself,
Then walked across the room, sat down, and cried;
He stalled midair, astounded on the shelf
Of that blue self,

Till paying out his rope and working down
He bumped to where he'd started off, loose ride
Back to the sidewalk, street, and vacant ground
Long his before he ever tried
Two intervening sides.

Then he was back, washing the mirrored blue
Of all he saw—within, the dollhouse walls
Of offices, and people passing through
To sometimes stop and answer calls
Then walk the halls.

Till now two lines spaghetti cross the top,
Sway back and forth, settle and descend,
Green paying out till red belays the stop,
And movement is a pendulum that ends
Where it begins:

Then he kicks off, swings back, pumps up momentum,
Fanning by so sometimes looking in
And sometimes out, thanks to the sky-blue sum
The glass has taught, reflecting him,
Silent and thin;

As some days all he thinks is frame to frame,
Cleaning until it seems there's no one there,
Nor glass between, but everything the same,
Till he has washed and dried the air
Of nowhere.

A Baseball Team of Unknown Navy Pilots, Pacific Theater, 1944

Assigned a week's good bunt, run, throw,
Makeshift uniforms, long practices,
Then games, playoffs, and a round of photos
Stark as this one slipping from its frame,
Where hats, gloves, bats in hand these stood
Lined up and focused, smiling and unnamed—

Till the shutter clicked and each went back,
Retracing zagged geometries
Of the navigator's elbowed tack
And smudged replotted overrule
Pulled from a fix when miles off track
They crabbed the wind and calculated fuel;

And then the wide sleek secret fleet below
Blacked out until the climbing tracers
Sent their bright concussive flak
And going on was all. Time wound,
And some planes banking, others not;
And the one, tail-riddled, easing down,

Crew tossing weight for altitude
Till smoke and someone spelling out a fix.
Then static graveling the words.
And still these faces, whose names we never got,
As all we know is they returned to bases,
Went up when told, came home or not.

Reading before We Read,
Horoscope and Weather

My father laughing over the morning paper
Where the written world fell open on the funnies,
Manic sports, stalled politics . . . and where
The Horoscope said, "now," the Forecast, "sunny,"

He couldn't laugh enough, so skipped a page,
Then another, till the back door shut,
An engine turned, and I woke up his age
In the mirror of a gray no-scissors cut.

He backed out of his pulling in at night
As light elbowed past an opened door, failing
Down six empty steps. Now a wall-switch bites
Blue sparks before the neon's billowing

Over another kitchen's white-on-white
Enameling; and now the sun is up
And climbing through the windows to a height
I follow out and off beyond the steep

Fence and trees to where the sky cuts flat
And blank as the paper spread in front of him,

My father then, waiting till I'd padded in, pulled out
My chair, inched up, and yawned that he begin.

Nothing is as funny now as then.
Still, when they rumple in, they bring his eyes
And mine, squinting and wet with laughing
Over the cracked, cracked up, sidewise, unwise

Stories that I read to them, telling how
We bend, break, wires shorting, knotting and strange;
Never as the Horoscope's predicted "now,"
But as the weather comes, fresh and ignorant of change.

Sequence

Sang off-key so mouthed the words,
Looked judicious when he couldn't hear,
What he forgot claimed he didn't need,
Avoided mirrors and biographies,
Read the sports and rarely finished,
Never listened but liked to talk.

Pushed when the door said Pull,
Eavesdropped on telephones,
Blew his nose on linen napkins;
Had a dog he couldn't call,
Built a house he didn't finish,
Had a job he never named,
Thought his father's life was sad.

Chewed rubber bands, sucked spaghetti,
Parked in handicapped slots,
Jammed the meter with slugs,
Backed without looking,
Braked on ice, and sometimes late at night
Drove on the wrong side laughing,
Laughing on the wrong side all the way home.

Zamboni's Law

Shave, water, scrub, and sweep the rink
Of all the etched meanderings
By which the skaters enter their
Broad cursives on the ice;
Play the music slow or play it fast,
Then turn the lights until you see
That only by Zamboni things agree.

Knife round and round the ice those O's
Whose widened emptiness controls
The way a skater's clockwise run
Gives out before the law.
Let tickets flood across the gates,
As now the skaters race to learn
All is erased when it's Zamboni's turn;

As now the slow-curved couples pass,
Nodding and talking, wobbling on,
And the overtaking singles
Pumping and weaving ahead,
Till coming round again they lean
Angled for that opening whose good
Is that Zamboni's law stands understood—

When the foghorn warning sounds its bass
Expelling each beyond the ice
So all stall mute outside the wall,
Watching how the blue, bulked, boxy grind
Restores a hardened glaze
As cold and clear as any thought we keep
To save Zamboni's law from how Zamboni sweeps.

Eyeing the World

Furtive the hedgerow cat
Crouched watchfully wise
At the field's far edge, as fat
As suspicious behind bright eyes

That study the rows
For rabbit and shrew, mouse or mole
Shrinking in shadows,
Wing-scything shadows that circle,

Descend, till the cat curls small
To see what follows—
The hawk's wings sprawled
As it tears, swallows,

A dark-phase bird
Wide over a shrew,
And eyeing the world
For anything new

In the casual field;
Till the hawk now done
Folds its wings, hops,
Flaps up, and climbs the sun;

Leaving the bones
And the cat's crouched wonder
At death's high ocean
Of light and hunger.

Coach

All trucks were from Hell and deserved my bite,
All children sheep and not to leave the yard.
Before I came, the house was unsafe;
The man whistled and no one heard,
And the huge trucks lumbered.

When the boy walked out, ball in hand,
I coached. He called me that. "Coach,"
He'd say, and I'd bark back, "Now! Now!"
Till the game was "Here Coach, Fetch Coach,"
And I was off and straightway back, unless,
Of course, one of the trucks from Hell passed by.

Thrown objects were my specialty,
The lazy sticks, their high trajectories,
That, and the knack I had for words—
Here, fetch, hunt, stay, sit, lie down . . .
And names, for the boy, his sister.
I lived those names twelve years, a diplomat
Who read the world four different ways,
Nose, ear, eye, and sometimes what was said.

When my coat thinned, legs stiffened, and I
Turned deaf, I was practical; I didn't run,
Limped wisely over, once the stick had plopped.
Then the children left, as sticks were lost,
As the man's whistle rose past hearing,
As all sounds stopped, and I was nose and eye,
Watching the trucks from Hell roll by,
Each silent and deserving of my bite,
Which the last one got, till I never let go.

The Razed House

Take the steep stairs up to where the rafters meet
And fan back down into the eaves
Like abstract tepees hung beneath
The ridgepole height and attic reach
Of a roof that hides what holds it up,
A maze of canted tensions,
King post, tie beam, purlin, strut.
Walk on the loosely slatted floor, testing
The syncopated clack and sway of beam one way
And unnailed plank the other, while beneath,
Calamitously poised, nested mice
Listen in the runneling snugs of the floor's dark length.

Or go three floors back down the way you climbed
To the burrowed basement darkening from sight,
Where the landing stalls and sunless slab
Opens on abandonment—corners cobwebbed
And flecked with wings on fretwork lines;
And beneath, here and there gnawed exits where
Rats stretch and wedge coaxial spines—
Sometimes a hole as circular and true
As if by template, yet empty as retreat;
And once, high in the wall, the delicate crest
Of a small skull, and ribs woven
In the briared lattice of an abandoned nest.

Between the scaled extremes of high and low
There's carpet and the polished wood
Of what you know, walking the average day
That voids its shadows—as the sprinkler goes,
A boy passes, arcs his paper, hears it plop,
And a dog wakes, collects his tongue, stands,
Stretches, watching a school bus yellow its stop,
Barged halt and flapping folding door
Till no one's there; and the wheels turn
And gears thrum, beyond the blue exhaust blown
Sideways and lingering like the spent gesture
Of a struck match, doused fire, someone alone.

Rise in the dark, pull on the clothes you wore
The day before, then pad out through the house,
Not seeing the table, chair, breakfront, sideboard
But sensing certain densities along a floor
You know by heart—till there's the rocker, stilled
And tilting back before the window where
The first light fills your sill,
And the yard resolves
Its terraced beds, edging into color
As though the green world woke restored again. As though.
And a car passes, lights pushing two white bowls
Of the concrete over which it rolls.

No architect comes after where you walk;
Only the rooms, whose walls are echoes of

A self-repeating voice that names its way
As if it made the woodwork talk.
But a nail, backed out from driven in,
Catches your sleeve as often as you pass;
Hammer it home, the wood will twist it out again.
And the windows, whose glass ripples and runs
Like water over glass, they stand
Immovably blank, neither cluttered nor clear,
Painted into their frames so the lattice holds
Two worlds at once—rooms you walk, and the yard's high air

In which the afternoon stretches overhead,
Filling the elbowed branching trees
As now you hear a few dry leaves
Blown edgewise scraping up the wall
Into the vaulted high of one hard gust
So circling they widen, drop. You know
The end is the end when the numbers change,
Phone and address; and never other name
But as you'd spell abandonment;
Till the walls come down and fill the basement up,
And the workers leave, some looking back, some not,
And you're a quiet sentence, a harbored thought.

Four Winter Flies

Lost and stumbling across the window,
They want the light that looks like warmth until
I lift the sash and off they go,
Blown in a brief cold gust that stuns, its chill

Leaving them slow to recover. Then they return,
Dotting the glass, tracing what they cannot touch
Until they're vacuumed up and out to turn
Into the earth for which they've swarmed so much.

May each buzz back behind its thousand eyes
To pace the unforgiving pane where sight
Said "come" and it could not and died,
As all die, opposite the world's long light

Whose bare-limbed seepage and shallowing rise
Once proved the brief ellipsis of four late flies.

Dog, Dog, Object, Object

Head lowered to his snuffling
After a sensed and senseless knowing
Of the grassy world where pattern's movement
And shape's the shadow of a shape,
He's found a trail, yanks after it,
Whimpers, runs, leash rising taut, then stops,
Turns, backtracks, catches up the way again
And is off again with a certainty I can't explain.

There is the long-tongued lap for water
And the wide-jawed, lounging tongue by which he sweats;
There is his three-turn-curling-down-to-sleep
And the stiff-legged, tail-up snarl and stare
That means beware; then the panting that is laughter,
Like his fanning tail's hello. These from the wild,
Whose language is bark, growl, howl, whine, yelp.

Then there's the thing that I have taught,
His long pull on the long lead towards what?
Mysteries require leads, and must have two to play.
Leaf mold, mildew, mull, and duff we go;
Some object lost, I tell him, "hunt," "hunt slow,"
Though knowing nothing's whereabouts.

And he is up circling, then setting out,
As though I'm right, as though the thing I say,
Without my knowing where, is really there.
Dog, Dog. A lowly newness takes the air;
Neither of us knowing why we go,
Just one believing so.

II

This

Gust blustering, and the March rain
Loosening its chill percussive tap
A thousand pockmarks up the drive,
Crossing where the silt dust gives to grass
So only sound—till that gone too,
As a single crow glides south-southeast,
Chasing some few bruised clouds on a wind
Plundering the low sky's crazy shapes,

And then the valance-down blue virga
Dropping from its shelf of clouds
And disappearing midway up,
As though by falling all might rise
And rising fall again above
The knuckling roots' blind budge
And mineral buckling out into
That web where mole and shrew will wait,

As now a new gust rolling through,
And the long rain reaching fully down,
Scattering and cold, mining the roof,
Runneling the yard, tenpenny hard
Its hammering hiss, saying, this, this, this.

The Pyromaniac

A one-story is disheartening,
Brief unelaborated light building
Under eaves, traveling sideways, gulping air,
And the slow smoke bellying after.
Three stories, four, five, or more work best
For my hushed start, in which the rest
Becomes a climbing fall toward light,
The blue flame's leap to furnace white
And stoked accumulation where
Hunger lives on hunger, hollowing air
As the dicing flames still time,
As empty coats, arms bent in pantomime,
Go up, as my two shoes tip up, their toes
Curled the way I make whole buildings go—
Out of the rich gas and fire's brief bright
Dancing its combustible light
On top of light, as if it drew
The nail-board-mortar of all lives into
One hot cumulus billowing from below.

That's why I strike the match, that I may know
No god's revenge for fire, but my own,
My own curled side bent to a stone

As obdurate and blank as hate,
Although not for some dark bird's appetite,
I have my own of that, instead the flame,
Consuming everything the same
Till nothing offers more of hope
Than gas-soaked rags, the building smoke
That hides its fire so rising whole
Bright tongues curl into coals
As air shafts roar and windows amplify
How high my hungry bright will bite the sky.

The Sorrows of Lester Buster

First there were the trips, the cars, then girls;
And following that an ennui like sap
Sticking to every sentence he unfurled,
His welling forth become her dripping tap

Till balding faster than he could gray,
He said he wanted his autonomy;
And so she let him go his way, away,
Not even asking alimony.

Then he returned, having grown, he said . . . and changed.
But she had got the habit of the feel
Of being free, though she offered to arrange
A separate room, trying to smile.

But he was ardently back, he said;
So she subscribed to the daily as his wife,
Frying his eggs, bacon, steaks, and skillet breads,
Freezing the desserts he liked about his life,

As along it went, his middle age,
Muddling on for a year or two,
Until she said, "All the world's a stage
You're passing through."

And he was, through that is, dead in the act,
In a motel on the edge of town—
No girl left, fictitious names for facts,
Only his old stiff self to pin him down.

Outside, the flashing lights went round and round
To the sirens, radios, phones, and the sound
Of cameras and the gurney unfolding,
Till someone took her arm and she was holding

A plastic bag with watch, wallet, ring.
"Can you identify these things?"
He wanted to know, "Were they, the, his, effects?"
She stood, as though waiting for the next

Installment. Later, some neighbors standing by
Saw her son pull up, hop out, get the door,
Then heard her say while waving them good-by,
"I think a little sooner's always better."

Recovery

That elbow with its pinpoint bruise
Just where the ligament tore loose,
Or herniated disk, pancaked sideways
And threatening to stay that way—
Till you're a sorry manikin for clothes,
Who bending stiffly down to hoist his bags
Stays put, until the comedy allows
That someone bend to bend you up again;

Then bone spur knuckled into nerve
So arm shoots pain and fingers numb,
Or spasm through the neck so head clocks down,
Stilled in rigid compensation;
Gimp knee, arthritic toe, a touch of gout,
And off you go, but differently,
Until, gout gone, you tiptoe after.

That is the mystery by which the late pain
Walks a later floor, answers each new step,
And punctuates tomorrow's tense,
As with a rib's caught breath, carved shape;
Or emphysema quantifying stairs,
Till every step's a calisthenic now
Collected on its miniature abyss—

Where the crooked elbow can't unbend
So arm goes only so much high,
Where the football knee that never kneels
Unhinges and rehinges equally,
Where winter-long the twisted spine perfects its coat,
As all my life I thought shape shrouded form
And form was full, but where we wince
As though called back we hollow how we go.

The God Doll

Up in the corner where you've put her,
A spider finger-walks its way
Over its web, retrieves a fly, then backs
The other way to eat and wait, wait and eat.
Later, what's left sags in the web's geometry.
Knocked down by broom, brush, tired dust cloth,
They reappear, the web and its trash, daily.

No matter how often you knock it down,
It reappears, that fragile geometric
Trap, treasure-rounding as the eye;
And whether you study the doll below
Or trace the slow-slung canopy above,
You only say the things you see:

Two chipped fingers, chinks where either arm
Came off; glued back, the glue's thin stain.
And then those fine cracks down-along the torso,
Some of them stretching to the knees,
Dividing into hairline fortunes;
Breakages or thin openings?
Either way, crookedly collaborative.

Stand back, then off to either side, the eyes
Follow, unseeing; they follow,
Like the doll's generalizing smile—
As the spider builds, catches, eats, then waits
For another fly whose thousand eyes will steer
Into the broken and composed geometry
Of a world lighter than the things it holds.

Grown Men at Touch

Of the barn's shadow we declared our field.
The ball, six to a side, and two-hand-touch
Went anywhere the barn's broad shadow stretched:
It grew flat wide out of the eastern side
All afternoon. By four, our shadow-field
Had gone long past the longest pass;
By five, no one could run its length.
Across the eastern grass the barn squared black
And increased as the sun sank low, so slant
Was all the light we had, and the long field
Longer still.
                    Play only means because it ends.
But here the field ran on, out to the next field
And the next, as shadow shaded into dark
So fences disappeared, roads sank, trees blanked.
And there was no way now to stop the game
In which one play means miles out through a night
That turns a stare blind wide of sight
With searching out the grown-up trick
By which you don't see and you never quit.

Since the Noon Mail Stopped

Once upon a time, when the clocks were slow
And windows tall with all I didn't know,
One thing confirmed the ordinary day
And taught me how the grown-up world would stay.

The mail fell from its secret in the door,
Silent and leaflike, loose along the floor,
And always someone gathered it from there,
Explaining all that *big* that came from *where*

As though each correspondence mapped a route
Beyond the origins of hidden doubt.
And of the ones who answered that address
Nothing's changed their opening from this:

Now that there's no delivery for here,
And those who've walked ahead have turned and stare,
I write the names for whom the letters drop
Unchanging where the noon mail stops.

Dantini

Inflated clown pajamas and a nose
Red golf-ball-round and teed-up-bright
Accompany the grease-paint sausage smile,
Which like the nose, long shoes (add wig and brows)
Curls up into incapable of down,
Even as he toes it on the wire, teeters,
Takes another step—lurch left, lurch right—
Then looking high, palms out and likewise up,
Goes slow-fall backwards over our assembled dark,

As even the stilt-man and midget halt,
Knife-thrower lowers his see-through blindfold,
Stops the wheel, unties his vertigo beauty
So the two stand holding hands and looking up

Where the clown's bent knee catches the wire
So head-down pendulum he swings
Until, leg wrapped, he rolls him rightly up,
Stands, looks out, sees he's facing wrong,
So head-down-under-knee turns all-way round;

But then he's down again, fist round the wire,
Two fists, till kicking out he chins it up

And, stomach V'd, head nodding down,
Cranks tight-round through three somersaults,
The last from which he's to his feet,
Hands out, accepting our applause,

As platformed now he bows the Big Top down,
And for the first time in his painted smile
He really smiles, teeth large, yellow, uneven,
Mouth widened on the picket dark of us,
Who also smile, smile up complicitly,
Wanting both conclusions, balance *and* fall.

Perverse of us. Manipulative of him?
Why not, when all economies tip so
It's this-one-up and that-one-down,
As we go on applauding all the gasps
He's caused; as though we understood for once
The generous proximity
Of one who makes up face and name,
Jugs high with low, then bows and waves;
Walks out, eyes level for the other side,
Walks out that way, or doesn't walk at all.

Late Fall, Late Light

As if an army rose out of one grave
Though not out of one wish but millions,
So looking back the landscape widened till
Each field became its own rich opening
Beside a round-top country road
Running its long down-backwards slowly home,

And the loose-leaf look of it, all afternoon,
Firing October's brilliant camouflage,
Holding the late light brighter where
It breaks between the rounding reds and yellows,
A thousand brief illuminated stops
So leaf to limb to trunk to undergrowth
The light collects in variegated shades
That deepen where they spread,
While overhead the round-eyed sky
That never blinks but eyes us blindly on
Goes on as bluely blank as ever,
Till the low sun levels through the trees,
Its thousand changes burning into one.

Golden

Over their piggy banks and good-luck charms
The ones who ought to know have flat forgot,
So go off calling each "Old What's-His-Name,"
While parking crookedly or idling through green.
These are the grown-out grown ups, going so's
You'd never guess the poverty they caved
With kissing the boss and feeding the plans
By which some actuary averaged hope
For the muzzy condo's lazy days
Kicked in once the retirement's had its way.

Wide afternoons of golf, or goofing off,
Reviving walks, odd talks—these do the trick;
It's little more than opening a door
For getting off or hauling it about
Now that the future's finally paying out.

Stick Builder

Hammer, nail, and board I go, pounding
Without blueprints so stud, joist, and rafter meet
As though I built by ear; stout hammering
And saw that say I know board feet
By the shapes they take, each room expanding
Six ways from two hands, until complete.
As now the whole house stands complete, waiting
Those who moving in will sleep and eat
Inside the idea I have built for them,
Which is as close as I will ever live to them.
That's why, finishing, I sign and say, "Stick Built." So
Someday cleaning out their attic they will know
Whose hand was here before there was a here,
Who built by touch so like touch he was near.

Etude on a Music Stand

Abstractly skeletal and waiting,
Dull nickel-shine unfolding up
Where the dutiful music spreads, curls,
This is the sad equivalence
Of upright for the printed sheet
And three prongs down for all the rest,
Such managing for so much same,
As though one score kept keeping score,
There where the chorus hollows halls,
And shallows on one self-sustaining chord,
As window-broken light, or shadowed turns,
As front rows empty darkly back,
And prodigy and glee and impresario
Imperceptibly the bow unfolds.

The Crows

There were the cautionary crows
Complaining tree to tree. He moved below,
Watching them lumber into the air,
Lifting and lighting, alone, in pairs,
Till lazing off in ragged echelons
They climbed, thinned from sight, and were gone—
As though the black of them were soluble,
Their outward empty wings as probable
As where he crouched, picking through the used,
Forgotten, broken, and refused
Collection of the entire town's slagged junk,
Last week already dozed and steeply sunk
But for a bookcase, couch, and chair
Piled near a bedstead heading up the air.

Across the way his leaning truck
Waited for the sum of what he'd lug,
Its cluttered bed already stacked with tires,
Shutters, axles, spools of wire.
But then he saw the high returning crows,
Lined up, stretched, lumbering and slow,
Till rounding down they tightened, dropped,
Opened, settled, heads cocked.

And then the one hopped up, the others flapped,
As they seesaw-walked it toward a strip
Of something only they could see.
Circling, they picked it patiently.

And the man forgetting what he held
And turning from the high truck's tilting load
Stepped sideways for a closer look—
One foot, another; till the crows spooked.
And all their metal voices rose,
Wings banking sideways out and low
As though they'd angle back for more,
Of what they found so rich before.

And he stood where he sized the ground.
Nothing. Bits of paper floating down,
Light scratch marks crisscrossed through the dust,
That momently blew nowhere in a gust;
Till bending close, pushing aside some trash
He saw the bones, dark hair, and ash.
Then he was in his truck and working gears
Ahead into the bug-flecked windshield's smear,
As farther back still stood the trees,
Motionless and black, shadowing degrees
By which the day went on beneath a sun
That only meant the sun, now that the crows were done.

III

Cold

Another front, sleet, snow, and the feeder
Leaning in a wind cranking from the north
And tanking coldly in all afternoon,
As I have carried seed and scattered seed,
Built piles of brush with more seed underneath,
While overhead and off to every side
The junkos, siskins, cardinals, thrashers wait
For my huffed pumping back indoors again:
Then the hushed world darting down, some gliding,
Others slipping sideways in to land, stand,
Go marching, cocked heads angling for seeds.

Until a storm of blackbirds clots the sky—
Huge clogged formations banking left and right,
Then darting low, skimming the limbs and gone,
As two large crows have folded in and walk
A black ellipse of seeds across the snow;
Till even the crows are up, rowing darkly,
And something larger circling above,
Its tipped wings widening with rounding down.

I watch the hedge where all the locals hide,
Limbs stitched so's not a cardinal's hood in sight,

As now the hawk glides in, bends, seizes a limb.
Another thirty minutes means full dark.

But then the hawk is off and up the wind,
Rising and banking, circling till gone,
And all the locals piling it back in,
So many reds and grays darting through limbs,
And something new, a goldfinch here, there; hidden.

As the light bleeds out along an angled shaft
The kitchen window throws across the snow
Where wing by wing the count ticks off to one
Gray junko hunched inside the feeder's base
And working through what's left so he can last
A night well on its way down under zero.
He rustles, kicks; the feeder twists.
I watch to see which way he'll fly. He stays—

And then it was so dark his flying went
Hiddenly beyond my looking out,
As suddenly the wind was all I said,
Above the window's light, flooding back the snow;
And farther, the feeder swaying emptily,
As gray to darker gray, to dark itself
Something had gone that I wished beyond reason.

Pictures from January

So many frames hung, and each an opening,
Till in the new house the old one punctures walls
With vague aunts, arrested uncles, glum cousins,
All posing by their upright rounded cars
And oafing it before the-house-before
With its bleached, high, implacably flat facade
Of a late-Victorian idea
Concerning angularity and space.

Years loom above collective poses,
The stalled, bland squinting smiles of relatives
Reduced to sequences, while prior to that,
At a depth of field the camera misses
The farm runs on unfolding into haze.
Meanwhile, today, each window, hall, or room
Becomes the place you stand and see
How still and oversized the past's become.

Sometimes a car grinds up the gravel drive
And rounds the eyelet circle, till facing down
The long shot to the highway where it turned
It brakes, stops, stands, and goes on idling;
While farther off a freight pounds out of town,

Its loose cars echoing and lost
In a whistle's high unanswerable fade.

Why recollect what's absolutely lost,
Walking a life out through its rooms
Of sixty years; why drag things up
So lenses magnify the sepias
Of a January light down through
A corridor that gradually turns dark?
And after that the driveway's round about,
From which two graveled tracks S down the yard
And fan into a road that curves from sight,
Till you're the slow steps lengthening the hall,
The deep-set backward monochrome of now.

The Tent

Too serious above his opened book,
Our father told us not to whisper a word,
So everything we said we had to shout,
As running for the phone and answering
With "She's out to the barn to milk the cows,"
Or "He's off with his mother sewing clothes,"
We'd hoof it up and down the hardwood hall,
Rip arguments, then pound the bedroom walls,
Stomp up and down the stairs, slam doors, bang drawers,

Until he came home with the tent from Sears
And, busying past every question why,
Scanned the instructions, arched them for the trash,
Then propped two poles and started pounding stakes.

So next the soft green boxy sag was up—
And the brand-new Coleman and folding chair;
Then for the two months left that summer
Our father finished dinner, walked outside,
Nursed the hissing Coleman up to bright,
And, opening the folding chair, took out his book.

At first our mother watched him from the door,
But then gave backwards to the living room
Where we now entered quietly.
At dusk, neighbors driving home slowed and stared
At the tent's green square and small white door,
Our father leaning forward in the light
As the high astringent failing sky bled dark
And underneath the tent glared on.

Back in the house we hoofed about more slowly,
Spoke less, and steered around our arguments,
Agreed to leave the TV volume low,
Quit dawdling and stumped to bed on time.

And never knew just when the lamp went out,
As silent in our sleep the back screen swung
First one way then the other, as whoever
Walked back in had decided he would stay.

A Display of Old Novels

Airtight and shaded so the light clocks right,
Their glass tops turn doubly reflective
When my stilled face lowers dumbly into view,
As looking down and reading through
The titles, I scan an opened page or two.

Here is a scene swells mighty over dinner,
While next the solemn narrator
Sums up the long before he can't quite say.
I read just long enough to learn
What it was he couldn't, then told us anyway.

And now there are the photographs,
Authors head-on or to one side,
But never from the back, the way
I slip up on them now, moving sideways,
Bowing and browsing the display.

Next time I'm here these pages will be gone,
But not for good just farther back,
Names and titles catalogued from view
As suits the storied distant few
Who got it right by living through

All the reasons reason fails at last,
The hero changes names and moves away,
Where rents are cheap and no one knows his past,
The minor furies trailing in like strays,
Happy for a handout, another day.

Census

Reduced from potency to act to fact,
They go about collecting the mail
And morning paper, paying bills,
Walking the dog or letting out the cat.

The close-cut grass and bordered garden plots,
And the houses from which these sometimes walk
And sometimes stop and wave as though to talk
Then, nothing said, survey their lots . . .

So stand the argyled laughable legs
Hairless under the fading plaids
Of sagged Bermudas, tented over sad
Bone-white knees balancing two waxed pegs

Sticking from their yards. Then going inside
These fade behind the paper's backward fold;
Till walking out again to move the hose,
Night rounds, they stay, and no one notices.

One by one, windows on the street click on,
Lights leading into shy recessive homes,
Or else the footlights to a dark which moves
As a silent giant stepping over lives.

Thaumatrope

And sometimes there's this parlor trick;
One side spider, other side the web,
Then thread pulled so the small card spins
And two sides turn to one.
                                        How obvious
And unrehearsed this seems, as darkened glass
Both mirrors and obscures, as pilots think
Blue water must mean bluer sky,
Till climbing up that unknown down
They enter their full-fathomed fall;

As though the world remained the world because
One seeing found the many ways agree—
The first six colors hidden in pastel,
Primary letters rounding into script,
As we have read the double agent's name
That buried in obits or in an ad
Was neither signature nor side.

Death by Metonymy

Nobody thought so, reading Zola to Bishop,
But now the bright blooms bob and choke
The low slant sedge and elbowed juniper.
"I like the lyrics, but the beat's too slow."
How much is grass before the landscape's green?
But who is going to extremes these days
When the average garden is proof. So say
You can build on that, as sometimes the sick do,
When they have over-planted hope,
Kept their seeds dry, waiting that season
When the green things turn leafy, tubular,
And moist, crowding for height, dying for light.

Set the table, sweep the floor, clean the sink;
And each was true; and you are through.

The Foliage Tour

I

We climb, the changes changing rapidly—
Tired greens, then yellows, orange, red, till green again;
"Forevergreen," says the man beside me;
Gauze for a cap and propped into a cane,
Raising his hand, touching where no hair remains.

He asks, "And what about your family?"
"In front," I point. We count three bobbing heads,
As the bus shifts down. And now it's up and slowly
Between the always evergreen he said—
Before we counted heads.

"And yours?" I ask mechanically.
"Just one, and she's gone on for now."
He says that carefully, studying me,
Waiting to hear me ask what I would know,
"Where did she go?"

But when I ask he only smiles,
Looking up the aisle as though the future tense
Climbed a road up through the fall for miles,
And no way left to stop, or turn the distance
To anything but distance.

2

Then we were coasting down the way we came,
Out of the evergreens, back to the range
Of red, orange, yellow—all different and the same,
As he was telling me the thing most strange
Was that the doctors changed.

So he checked out and started out,
Touring on the hope, or the belief in hope,
That he was well, "up and about,"
He said, "well as before; cresting slopes
And never out of rope."

Rope raveling like reason on a guess
And never any word for loss
Except percentages—more, less,
Maybe a few months more, dice tossed
And the odds at any cost . . .

As we, ticketed, bussed, and bland,
Became the road and whining wheels beneath
The ticking trees whose fractions were the land
We rode to see, all colors one, leaves and a leaf,
Shadow and belief.

The Funerals

You'd think we'd have them down by now,
Dark suits and all that driving back and forth
And walking in and walking out again
With hearing yet another's lost his lines
Somewhere inside the never-plot's last turn
Where "good show" equals "dumb show" equals "end."

Instead, there's but the low sun through the door,
And the sundial floor telling what comes next,
As tile-by-tile the light grows long beneath
We solemn few who fill the rows and watch
Our shadows climb the wall's blunt vertical,
Where later on it does no harm that when
We size the stone on which the last word's etched
We mind the light and skip the epitaph.

Mulligrubs and Mumbles

For Heather and Ian

To dance well or write a song
Is to admit that, however long,
Time works in ways that please,
Though *now* has notions up its sleeve,
So lunatic and wiseone meet
In the same mirror, take the same street
Down which to run away
Is crookedly to stay.

You're born to mulligrubs and mumbles,
A family of post-Cartesian grumblers;
Storm out without the credit card or keys,
You'll storm back in, to laughter by degrees,
Where the best divisions go by whole,
As the years will have us soul by soul,
As anyone who leaves begins
And welcome makes an end.

Driving the Christmas Lights

Having our neighborhood down by heart,
We set out for a larger look
Among the Christmas lights, which meant
To brighten, cheer, or merely decorate,
Hang easily enough that of them one may say
They do no harm and meanwhile brighten the eye.
    We drive. First there's Broad, then Main,
Then Dolphin, Buena Vista, Broad again,
While overhead a phosphorescent sky
Hangs muzzy as a bunched up comforter
Tossed out yet never opening,
A pastel cotton heft half-spread
And giving back, again, the Christmas lights.
    Inside our car the heater builds
A lower latitude: fogged windows clear;
The radio bells out with caroling.
Meanwhile the streets run one-way, sometimes two,
While, either way, our heads round after,
Catching the lights, pearled branches of evergreen,
The blinking O's of bright suspended wreaths,
Stalled reindeer, bloated Santas smiling, waving.
    And then a Greek Revival church juts up
Over a crèche with living animals

Tethered where they stand, mute and still beneath
A carillon that chimes out stereo,
In echoes syncopated and never catching up.
And now more houses, with lights outlining
Their cubes and A-frames, stalled gestures
That, drawn as brightly dotted cut-outs,
Show where the holes are opening
On families gone sleeping down within.

   But then we're driving out beyond the town,
Wide of all houses, lights, and lawns,
As up ahead briefly the moon breaks through,
A searchlight shaft of chalk-white stringent bright,
Then disappears, and we have topped a ramp,
Drifted left into a lane, and gathered speed,
Taking the long, wide circle route,

   Lights pointil in their distances
And all the little darks between,
The eyelet, button hole, or naught
Of what we cannot see, that other side
Of neuron and tungsten, its white-hot building
Incandescent-down to glint, following us
Like something suddenly alive, watchful, winking,

   As through an insect's thousand eyes
Where everything imagined, made, and given light
Spins out along its own cold multiple,
Spins, recedes, goes on unchanged—
Years from where the white-hot elements began,

Fixing all we've said or thought to say,
Did or left undone, picked up or dropped,
Gave, took, gave up, left, lost, discovered,
All the almost flash and frame of us,
The red now, green now, blue by which we go.

Band Day

Zinnias lean; mums fade, buckle;
October's flowers twist and elbow down,
And where the long light silhouettes a wall
Five kindred maples brighten into height.
Later, wind, and red leaves funneling
In contoured eddies over the yard
Until a minor piedmont builds

By which one solemn couple walks,
She pushing so the stroller's wheels
Bump up and caster down the side-
walk's slanting cracked and crooked slabs
As bald head nodding short affirmatives
Her husband goes on telling her
Whatever he is telling her.

They pass, she leaning sideways out
To look beneath the fringed and tilted top
Where now another bald head's pendulum
Goes on agreeing from below,
As rocking back and forth it weighs its arc
Of plumb-bob sway and settling
Over the up-down-broken way
The sidewalk makes of where it goes.

And the two bald heads continuing
The syncopated certainty
The sidewalk angles underneath,
While standing at the curb beside the car
And troubling odd pockets after keys
I hear a band off down the street
And watch the couple slow, stop, turn,

Then bring the stroller round and wait.
And drum major and majorettes
Now kicking through the outer reaches
Of the leaves, band tightened into ranks
Of red, gold, black, and mirrored brass,
And blaring down the street, until the whole
Commotion's going past. Then there's a gap,

The music shifts, and next another band;
As in between I watch the parents
Watching this, laughing, applauding all passing,
While underneath the stroller's tilted top,
Silent as a man knocked out of breath,
A small white head tips back, mouth wide,
Hands jerking up convulsively,

Until both bands diminish down the street
And one high lilting cry rises,
As though all sound continued in

A thin suspended voice through which
The long leaf-colored light came magnified
In absences blown down the empty street,
Where now the mother bends with gathering,

As if for once all we called beautiful
Lifted in a gust and slant of light
Along the settled, tilting, cracked way home
That these three take, facing silently
To where the faint notes echo, fade, go on.

Poetry Titles in the Series

John Hollander, *"Blue Wine" and Other Poems*
Robert Pack, *Waking to My Name: New and Selected Poems*
Philip Dacey, *The Boy under the Bed*
Wyatt Prunty, *The Times Between*
Barry Spacks, *Spacks Street: New and Selected Poems*
Gibbons Ruark, *Keeping Company*
David St. John, *Hush*
Wyatt Prunty, *What Women Know, What Men Believe*
Adrien Stoutenberg, *Land of Superior Mirages: New and Selected Poems*
John Hollander, *In Time and Place*
Charles Martin, *Steal the Bacon*
John Bricuth, *The Heisenberg Variations*
Tom Disch, *Yes, Let's: New and Selected Poems*
Wyatt Prunty, *Balance as Belief*
Tom Disch, *Dark Verses and Light*
Thomas Carper, *Fiddle Lane*
Emily Grosholz, *Eden*
X. J. Kennedy, *Dark Horses*
Wyatt Prunty, *The Run of the House*
Robert Phillips, *Breakdown Lane*
Vicki Hearne, *The Parts of Light*
Timothy Steele, *The Color Wheel*
Josephine Jacobsen, *In the Crevice of Time: New and Collected Poems*
Thomas Carper, *From Nature*
John Burt, *Work without Hope*
Josephine Jacobsen, *The Edge of the Sea: Collected Stories*
Charles Martin, *What the Darkness Proposes*

Wyatt Prunty teaches in the English Department at the University of the South and directs the Sewanee Writers' Conference. He is the author of five earlier volumes of poetry—*Domestic of the Outer Banks; The Times Between; What Women Know, What Men Believe; Balance as Belief;* and *The Run of the House*—the last four of which were published by the Johns Hopkins University Press. His other works include a critical study of contemporary poetry, *"Fallen from the Symboled World": Precedents for the New Formalism,* published in 1990.

Library of Congress Cataloging-in-Publication Data

Prunty, Wyatt.
    Since the noon mail stopped / Wyatt Prunty.
        p.   cm. — (Johns Hopkins, poetry and fiction)
        ISBN 0-8018-5646-9 (acid-free paper)
        I. Title.   II. Series.
    PS3566.R84S56   1997
    811'.54—dc21
                                      97-4993
                                        CIP

HOUSTON PUBLIC LIBRARY

R01056 50465

HUMCA   811
         P972

PRUNTY, WYATT
    SINCE THE NOON MAIL
STOPPED

5/08

HUMCA   811
         P972

Friends of the
Houston Public Library

HOUSTON PUBLIC LIBRARY
CENTRAL LIBRARY

SEP 97